Date: 11/1/12

J 797.21 ROM
Romanek, Trudee.
Splash it swimming /

PALM BEACH COUNTY
LIBRARY SYSTEM
3650 SUMMIT BLVD.
WEST PALM BEACH, FL 33406

Splash it Swimming

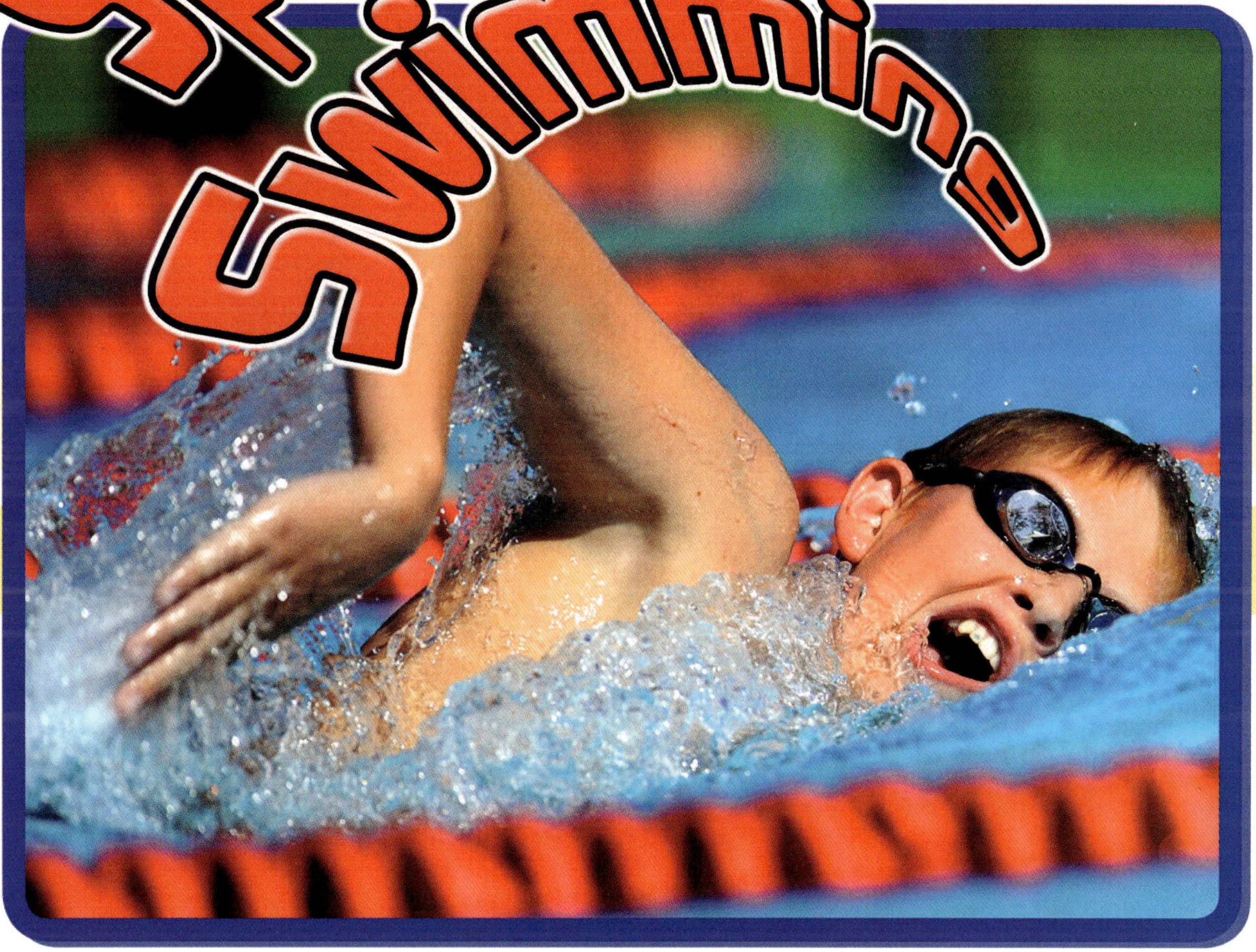

Trudee Romanek

Crabtree Publishing Company

www.crabtreebooks.com

Sports Starters
Created by Bobbie Kalman

Author
Trudee Romanek

Editors
Molly Aloian
Kathryn White

Proofreader
Kathy Middleton

Photo research
Melissa McClellan

Design
Tibor Choleva
Melissa McClellan

Production coordinator
Margaret Amy Salter

Prepress technician
Margaret Amy Salter

Print coordinator
Katherine Berti

Consultant
Martin Richard, Director of Communications for Swimming Canada

Illustrations
Leif Peng: page 9

Photographs
Corbis: © Franck Seguin/TempSport (p 29 top)
Dreamstime.com: © Chris Schmid (titlepage, p 11); © John Wollwerth (toc page); © Susan Leggett (p 7 left); © Patrick (p 7 right); © Shariff Che' Lah (p 12); © Endostock (p 15 bottom); © Peter Muzslay (back cover, p 17 top); © Nikita Sobolkov (p 17 bottom); © Wong Hock Weng John (p 24); © Susan Leggett (p 27); © Sarah Dusautoir (p 28); © Lunamarina (p 31 top)
iStockphoto.com: © Bob Thomas (p 10); © technotr (pp 23, 25); © Grady Reese (p 30 bottom); © kali9 (p 30 top)
Shutterstock.com: © Aleksandr Markin (p 4); © Sergey Peterman (front cover, p 13 top); © BrunoRosa (pp 13 bottom, 29 bottom); muzsy (p 14); © Iurii Osadchi (p 21); © Gert Johannes Jacobus Vrey (p 22); © Gorilla (p 26); © Zina Seletskaya (p 31)
Thinkstock: Ryan McVay, Photodisc (p 8); iStockphoto (pp 5, 15 top, 19); © Getty Images (pp 6, 15, 18, 20)

Created for Crabtree Publishing by BlueApple*Works*

Library and Archives Canada Cataloguing in Publication

Romanek, Trudee
    Splash it swimming / Trudee Romanek.

(Sports starters)
Includes index.
Issued also in electronic format.
ISBN 978-0-7787-3163-4 (bound).--ISBN 978-0-7787-3163-4 (pbk.)

    1. Swimming--Juvenile literature. I. Title.
II. Series: Sports starters (St. Catharines, Ont.)

GV837.6.R65 2012   j797.2'1   C2012-900883-4

Library of Congress Cataloging-in-Publication Data

Romanek, Trudee.
    Splash it swimming / Trudee Romanek.
        p. cm. -- (Sports starters)
    Includes index.
    ISBN 978-0-7787-3152-8 (reinforced library binding : alk. paper) --
ISBN 978-0-7787-3163-4 (pbk. : alk. paper) -- ISBN 978-1-4271-8850-2
(electronic pdf) -- ISBN 978-1-4271-9753-5 (electronic html)
    1. Swimming--Juvenile literature. I. Title.

GV837.6.R65 2012
797.2'1--dc23

2012004073

Crabtree Publishing Company

www.crabtreebooks.com   1-800-387-7650

Printed in the U.S.A./032012/CJ20120215

Copyright © **2012 CRABTREE PUBLISHING COMPANY**. All rights reserved. No part of this publication may be reproduced, stored in a retrieval system or be transmitted in any form or by any means, electronic, mechanical, photocopying, recording, or otherwise, without the prior written permission of Crabtree Publishing Company. In Canada: We acknowledge the financial support of the Government of Canada through the Canada Book Fund for our publishing activities.

Published in Canada
Crabtree Publishing
616 Welland Ave.
St. Catharines, Ontario
L2M 5V6

Published in the United States
Crabtree Publishing
PMB 59051
350 Fifth Avenue, 59th Floor
New York, New York 10118

Published in the United Kingdom
Crabtree Publishing
Maritime House
Basin Road North, Hove
BN41 1WR

Published in Australia
Crabtree Publishing
3 Charles Street
Coburg North
VIC 3058

Contents

What is swimming?	4
Gearing up	6
At the pool	8
Different strokes	10
Bobbing breaststroke	12
Beautiful butterfly	14
Take it back	16
Go the distance	18
All together now!	20
Ready, set, GO!	22
Rules of the race	24
Competition	26
Swimming stars	28
Dive in!	30
Glossary and Index	32

What is swimming?

Swimming is a sport that takes place in water, such as in a pool or lake. Swimmers move through the water by pulling with their arms and kicking their legs. The combinations of different arm and leg movements are called **strokes**. Swimming races are measured in meters. Races may be as short as 50 meters (164 feet) or as long as 1500 meters (4921 feet).

Swimmers must find time to breathe in between their strokes.

Olympic-size pools are 50 meters (164 feet) in length.

One or more

In most races, individual swimmers race against each other. Competitors swim beside each other in different lanes, which are long, narrow strips of the pool.

Some races are **relays** between teams that have four swimmers each. Every team member takes a turn swimming one part of the race.

Gearing up

All you really need to swim is a swimsuit. Swimmers who compete wear goggles to keep pool water out of their eyes. Most competitive swimmers wear a swim cap to keep their hair out of the way. The cap also makes a person's head smoother so it can slip through the water faster.

Swimmers wear goggles to see under water during every part of the race.

Super suits

Competitive swimmers wear swimsuits designed to slide easily through the water. They are tight-fitting suits with no flaps or ruffles to catch in the water. Some are made of special woven material.

Most swimmers who compete have a favorite type of suit for racing.

At the pool

Most pools that are used for swimming races are at least two meters (6 feet 7 inches) deep.

Floating **buoy lines** divide the pool into eight swimming lanes. Swimmers can see black lines on the bottom of their lanes and flags above their lanes. Lines and flags help swimmers tell when they are getting close to the pool's wall at the end of their lanes.

Long or short

There are two kinds of pools for international competitive swimming. Short-course pools are 25 meters (82 feet) long. Long-course pools are 50 meters (164 feet) long. Olympic swimming events take place in long-course pools.

Hey, coach!
Coaches help swimmers train and improve their strokes and race times. A coach's other important job is to encourage the swimmers to do their best.

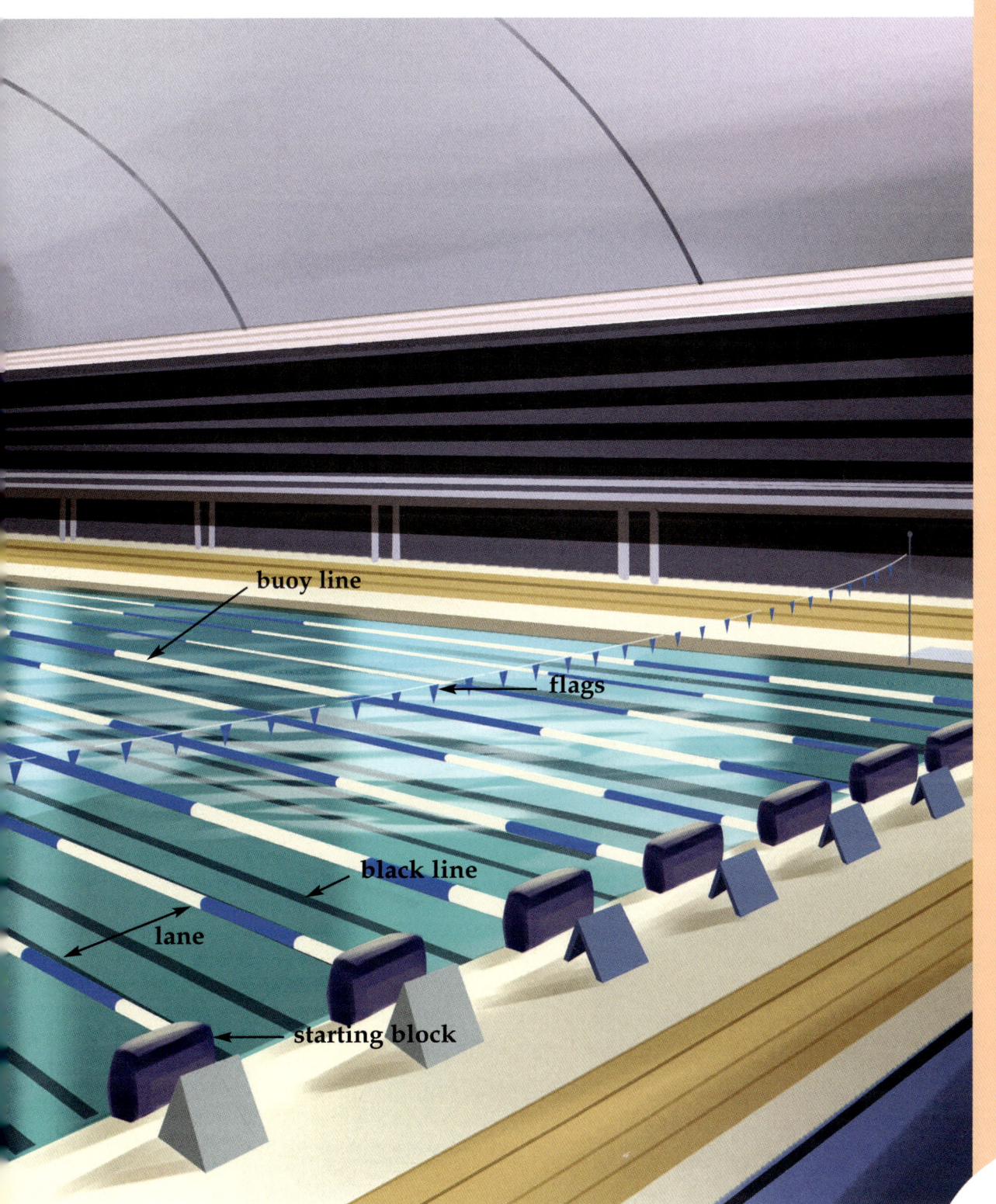

Different strokes

The **front crawl**, also known as freestyle, is the most popular swimming stroke. Front-crawl swimmers are facedown in the water. They **flutter kick** their legs, which means they kick their legs up and down one at a time. Swimmers also swing their arms in a pinwheel motion. While one arm goes down into the water, the other arm comes up from behind.

In the front crawl, the arms take turns slicing through the water.

Front-crawl swimmers turn their heads to breathe in.

New name

Every competition has **freestyle** races. This means swimmers can use any stroke they want. Swimmers usually use the front crawl because it is the fastest stroke. That is why the front crawl is now often called "freestyle."

Bobbing breaststroke

For this stroke, swimmers are also facedown in the water. They reach their hands forward and give a strong **frog kick** with their legs. Then they pull their arms back through the water and bob their heads up. They alternate these movements—kick then bob up, kick then bob up—until they reach the end of the pool.

These swimmers take a breath as they bob up.

Swimmers put their heads under the water after they bob up.

Take a deep breath

Some breaststroke swimmers breathe every time they bob up out of the water. Others breathe on every second or third bob so they can go faster.

Breaststroke swimmers breathe out when their heads are under the water.

Beautiful butterfly

This stroke is something like the breaststroke, but more complex. Many say it is the toughest stroke to do well.

The butterfly is another facedown stroke. In butterfly a swimmer's legs and body move together in a waving motion called a **dolphin kick**. The swimmer bursts forward, up and out of the water. The arms move, too. They swing out of the water behind the swimmer, then overhead to plunge down in front again.

The butterfly stroke takes a lot of energy and is very good exercise.

Doing the butterfly strengthens the chest and shoulder muscles, as well as the arms and legs.

Getting it right

It takes hard work and good coordination to get all the parts moving at the right time for this stroke!

The butterfly stroke gets its name from the swimmer's wide-open arm position.

Take it back

To swim the backstroke, a swimmer lies on his or her back facing up. The swimmer's arms move in a kind of backward pinwheel motion. One at a time, each arm comes up beside the leg and then out of the water, swinging back over the head. Each arm then pushes the water down beside the swimmer's body. His or her legs flutter kick the same way as in the front crawl.

A good start makes for a stronger race. This coach times her swimmer's backstroke start.

Breathing is easier doing the backstroke since your face is out of the water.

Swimming blind

One tricky thing about the backstroke is that you cannot see where you are going! Swimmers watch for the flags hanging above the water. When they see the flags, they know how many more strokes it will take before they reach the wall.

17

Go the distance

There are swimming races for all four of these strokes. The shorter races are 50 meters, 100 meters, and 200 meters. There is also a 400-meter race for only freestyle. For most races, swimmers must swim the length of the pool more than once. Each length is called a **lap**.

How many laps?
This chart shows how many laps you must swim for each race.

100 m = 2 laps

200 m = 4 laps

400 m = 8 laps

800 m = 16 laps

1500 m = 30 laps

In many open-water races, the crowd of swimmers start all together from the shore.

The long haul

Some races are longer. The Olympics and some other competitions include a women's 800-meter race and a men's 1500-meter race. There are also longer, open-water swims. These take place in a lake, ocean, or bay rather than a pool. A 5 km open-water race is a distance of about three miles. Other common lengths are 10 km, as in the Olympics, or 25 km.

All together now!

Some swim events are for teams of four swimmers. In the 4x100-meter freestyle relay, each teammate takes a turn swimming two laps in a long-course pool. There is also the 4x200-meter freestyle relay.

One team event involves all four strokes. In the 4x100-meter **medley** relay, the first swimmer swims two laps of backstroke in a long-course pool. The second teammate swims breaststroke and the third swims butterfly. The last swimmer on each team swims 100 meters of front crawl.

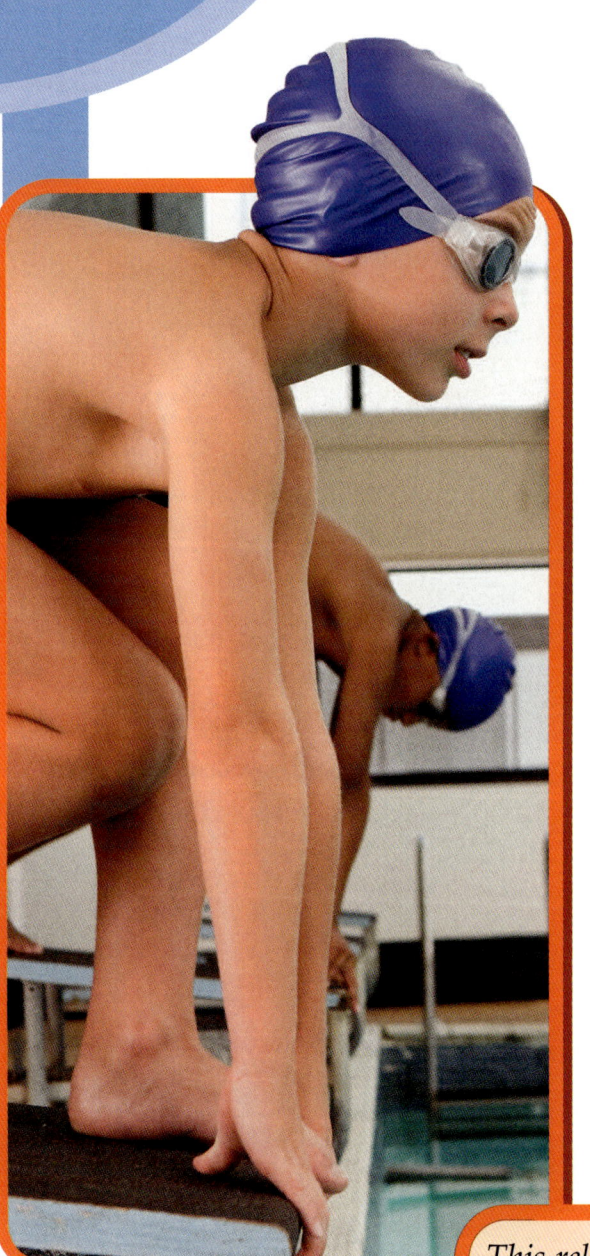

This relay swimmer waits to swim his part of the race.

Breaststroke is the third stroke in the IM.

Doing it all

For the individual medley, or IM, a swimmer swims all four strokes. In the 200-meter IM competitors swim one lap of each stroke in a long-course pool. They swim two laps of each for the 400-meter IM.

Ready, set, GO!

When the horn sounds, these backstroke swimmers will push off to start their race.

A whistle blows. Eight swimmers step up onto the **starting blocks**. "Take your marks," calls the referee. The swimmers bend down. Then a horn sounds, and they dive in! That is how most swim races begin.

Backstroke races start in the water. Swimmers hold a bar under the starting blocks with their feet on the wall of the pool. When the horn sounds, they let go and push off the wall with their feet.

Twists and turns

Most swim races are longer than one lap. When a swimmer gets near the end of a lap, he or she does a **tumble turn,** or flip turn. This flips the swimmer around the right way to swim back.

The tumble turn is like a summersault under water.

Pushing off from the wall gives the swimmer extra power for the next lap.

Rules of the race

Competitive swimming is all about speed. The fastest swimmer wins. Each swimmer is timed from when he or she leaves the start until that swimmer's hand touches the pool wall at the end of the race.

The first swimmer back to touch the wall wins!

A relay swimmer must wait for her teammate to touch before she dives in.

Staying in the game

There are some rules swimmers must follow. They must touch the pool at the end of each lap. They are not allowed to walk on the bottom of the pool or push off of it. Swimmers must swim most of the race on the water's surface. Swimming too far underwater is also against the rules. A swimmer can be **disqualified** from a race if he or she breaks these rules.

Competition

Like many athletes, swimmers are ranked according to how they compare with other swimmers. These **rankings** are based on each swimmer's best race times in previous competitions. Race times are often measured to the nearest one hundredth of a second!

Swimmers must do well in many races to get the chance to compete in the biggest swim meets. The Olympics, the World Aquatics Championships, and the Pan Pacific Games are a few of the most important meets.

Improving your own times can be as rewarding as winning.

Races give swimmers a chance to find out if their training has made them faster.

In the fast lane

For many races, organizers place the swimmers with the fastest times in the two center lanes of the pool. The next two fastest go in the next two lanes and so on.

Swimming stars

Today's young swimmers look up to champions such as American Michael Phelps. In 2004 at the Olympics in Athens, Greece, Michael Phelps won an incredible six gold and two bronze medals. In the next Olympic Games in Beijing, China, he took home eight golds.

With 14 gold medals, Michael Phelps holds the record for most Olympic gold medals won by an individual in any sport.

Great swimmers of the past include Americans Mark Spitz and Matt Biondi, Inge de Bruijn of the Netherlands, Alexander Popov of Russia, and Roland Matthes of Germany. Other long-time champions of the pool are Australian Ian Thorpe and American Natalie Coughlin.

Australia's Ian Thorpe became the youngest world champion at age 14.

Today's stars include Americans Ryan Lochte and Rebecca Soni, who won Male and Female Swimmers of the Year in 2010 and 2011, China's Sun Yang, and Federica Pelligrini of Italy.

In 2009, Federica Pelligrini became the first woman to swim the 400 m freestyle event in under four minutes.

Dive in!

Whether you are racing in the pool or paddling in a lake, swimming can be a lot of fun. Many communities and schools have swim teams. Local pools usually have swim times when anyone can swim. Most pools also have classes for those who want to learn and improve.

Swimming is terrific exercise. It strengthens many different muscles in your arms, legs, and body. It is also a great way to keep your heart and lungs healthy.

Get out and have fun swimming!

Glossary

Note: Boldfaced words that are defined in the text may not appear in the glossary.

buoy lines The strings of floats on the pool that separate the lanes

disqualified No longer allowed to win the race

dolphin kick A swimming movement in which the legs move as one unit

flutter kick A swimming movement of alternating leg kicks

freestyle A race in which swimmers use their choice of stroke

frog kick A swimming kick in which the legs move out to the sides

lap One length of a pool

medley A swim race that involves more than one kind of stroke

ranking The measure of how fast a swimmer is compared to other swimmers

relay A race in which teammates take turns swimming

starting block The small platform that a swimmer dives from to begin the race

stroke A set of arm, leg, and body swimming movements

tumble turn A flip that swimmers make at the end of the pool to turn and swim back

Index

backstroke 16, 17, 20, 22
breaststroke 12, 13, 14, 20, 21
breathe 4, 11, 12, 13, 17
buoy lines 8
butterfly 14, 15, 20
coaches 8
coordination 15
disqualification 25
dolphin kick 14
flags 8, 17
flip turn 23

flutter kick 10
freestyle 10, 11, 18, 20, 29
frog kick 12
front crawl 10, 11, 16, 20
individual medley 21
lanes 5, 8, 27
lap 18, 20, 21, 23, 25
medley 20, 21
muscles 4, 15, 30
Olympics 5, 8, 19, 26, 28
open-water races 19
Pelligrini, Federica 29

Phelps, Michael 29
rank 26
relay 5, 20, 25
rules 24, 25
speed 24
starting block 22
swimsuit 6, 7
teams 5, 20, 30
Thorpe, Ian 29
tumble turn 23